CHESTER RACCOON
and the
ALMOST PERFECT
SLEEPOVER

By Audrey Penn

Illustrated by
Barbara L. Gibson

Tanglewood • Indianapolis, IN

To my sister, Kathy Lefco
who let me go first.
And for Rabbi Stan, who didn't.
-A.P.

Published by Tanglewood Publishing, Inc.
Text © 2017 Audrey Penn
Illustrations © 2017 Barbara L. Gibson

Cover Design by Andrew Arnold • Interior Design by Amy Alick Perich

Tanglewood Publishing, Inc., 1060 N. Capitol Ave., Ste. E-395, Indianapolis, IN 46204 • www.tanglewoodbooks.com

Printed in U.S.A.
10 9 8 7 6 5 4 3 2 1

ISBN 978-1-939100-11-5

Library of Congress Cataloging-in-Publication Data

Names: Penn, Audrey, 1947- author. | Gibson, Barbara, illustrator.
Title: Chester Raccoon and the almost perfect sleepover / by Audrey Penn ;
   illustrated by Barbara L. Gibson.
Description: Indianapolis : Tanglewood, [2017] | Summary: "Chester Raccoon
   goes to his first sleepover and enjoys a day of fun and games with his
   friends. But when it is time to go to sleep, Chester feels his mother's
   love through his Kissing Hand, but still misses his home. Chester goes
   home and Mrs. Raccoon assures him he came home at just the right time"--
   Provided by publisher.
Identifiers: LCCN 2016044580 | ISBN 9781939100115 (hardback)
Subjects: | CYAC: Sleepovers--Fiction. | Raccoon--Fiction. | Nocturnal
   animals--Fiction. | Forest animals--Fiction. | BISAC: JUVENILE FICTION /
   Social Issues / New Experience. | JUVENILE FICTION / Bedtime & Dreams. |
   JUVENILE FICTION / Animals / Nocturnal. | JUVENILE FICTION / Holidays &
   Celebrations / Birthdays.
Classification: LCC PZ7.P38448 Chc 2017 | DDC [E]--dc23
LC record available at https://lccn.loc.gov/2016044580

Chester Raccoon hopped and skipped and bounced on his way to Pepper Opossum's tree for his very first sleepover.

"Are we almost there?" he asked his mother. "Will we get there soon?"

"Do you see that tall white oak on the far side of Butterfly Pond?" asked Mrs. Raccoon.

"Uh-huh."

"Well, that's where we're going."

A few minutes later, Chester and his mother were standing by the Opossum's tree.

"Have fun at your *overday*," Mrs. Raccoon told Chester. "I'll pick you up the moment the sun sets." She nuzzled his ear and kissed him right in the middle of his palm.

Chester squeezed his fingers around his mother's
Kissing Hand and felt her love and warmth all over.
But when she turned and walked away, the little
raccoon felt nervous and excited, all at the same time.
This was his first whole day away from home.

"Let's go have some fun," Mrs. Opossum told him.

Chester followed her up the tree to the lowest branch facing Willow Creek. Pepper Opossum and several of Chester's other friends were already there.

"We're hanging upside down by our tails," Pepper called.

"I can tell," laughed the little raccoon. He tiptoed over Pepper's long pink tail, Stanley Squirrel's fluffy gray tail, and Badger's thick brown tail, and then hung upside down between his best friend, Cassie Raccoon, and Sassafras Skunk. Amber Porcupine hung farther down the limb.

"This is fun!" Chester told Pepper. "The whole world is upside down."

"What's that smell?" grumbled Badger.
"Pee-yew!"

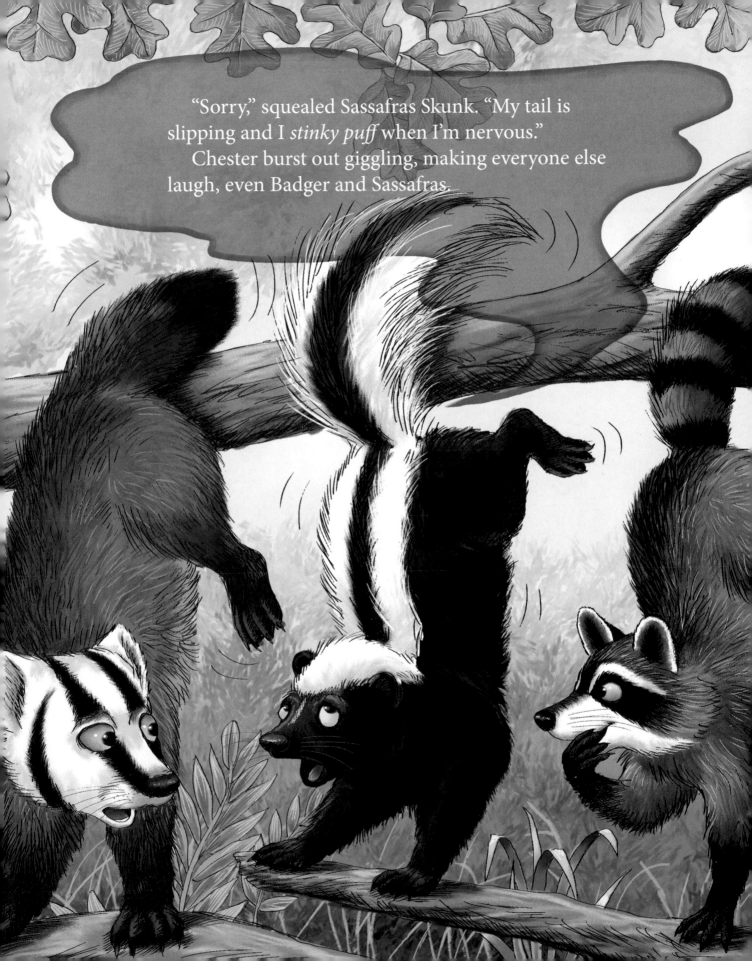

"Sorry," squealed Sassafras Skunk. "My tail is slipping and I *stinky puff* when I'm nervous."

Chester burst out giggling, making everyone else laugh, even Badger and Sassafras.

"Let's play Follow The Leader!" said Pepper,
jumping to the ground. "I get to be leader!"

Chester got in line and jumped when the
opossum jumped.

He ran around the maple tree when the
opossum ran around the maple tree.

And he splashed through Willow Creek, walked across a hollow log, and rolled down a bumpy, dusty hill until he was dizzy, and giggling, and covered in dirt, just like Pepper Opossum.

"Oh, Sassafras!" cried Stanley Squirrel.
"Sorry," chittered the little skunk. "I always *stinky puff* when I giggle."

"Let's play darts!" proposed Amber Porcupine. "Pull a quill from my tail and put an acorn on the sharpest end so it will fly like a dart."

"Won't that hurt you?" worried Chester.

"No," smiled Amber. "It only hurts if I get stuck."

"Please be careful with those pointy quills!"
Mrs. Opossum warned the children.
"We will!" everyone promised.

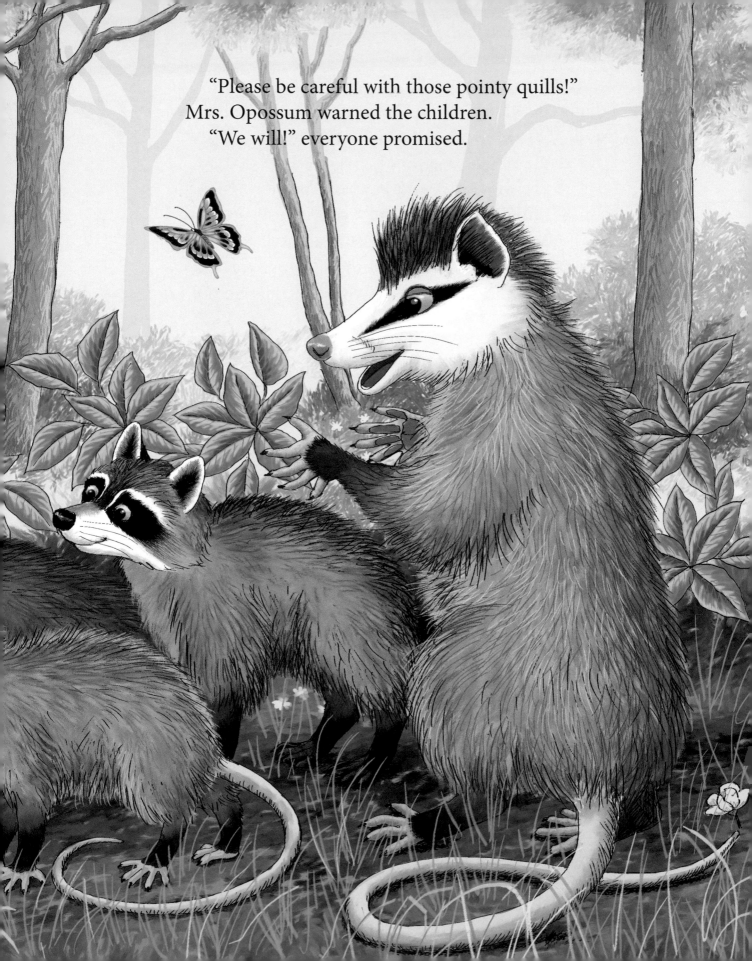

After everyone had their dart, and after everyone thanked Amber for the use of her tail quills, Pepper said, "Let's see whose dart goes the farthest. It's my overday, so I get to go first!"

"You're the host!" said Pepper's mother. "Do you think it might be politer to let your guests go first?"

"I guess so," the little opossum sighed.

Chester saw how disappointed Pepper was and asked, "Would you like to throw your dart before I do?"

Pepper's face lit up like a full moon. "We can throw them together!"

So Pepper and Chester threw their darts into the sky and watched them fly. The two quills landed side by side.

"Hurray!" shouted everyone. "It's a tie!"

Chester and Pepper high-fived.

Mrs. Opossum collected the sharp quills and put them safely away then returned with some favorite snacks.

Chester's eyes popped when he saw the bark plate filled with rotten fruits, nuts, and dead bugs, and the bird's nest bowl crawling with grubs and slugs!

"This is delicious!" mumbled Chester as he crunched a cricket between his teeth.

After snacks, Chester went with his friends to
Willow Creek where he caught minnows and let
them go and then skipped stones across the water.

"Oh, Sassafras!" cried everyone.

"I'm sorry," yawned the little skunk. "I *stinky puff* when I'm sleepy."

"I'm sleepy, too," yawned Badger and Stanley and Amber.

"So are we," confessed Chester and Cassie.

And though it was still early in the overday, even Pepper admitted he was all tuckered out.

YAWN!

Soon everyone was curled up and fast asleep in the
opossum's hollow—everyone but Chester Raccoon.
He laid awake and pressed his mother's Kissing
Hand to his cheek. He felt her love and warmth
all around him. And he wasn't afraid to sleep in
opossum's hollow. But it wasn't *his* hollow.

Chester missed sleeping across from his brother Ronny. He missed sleeping beneath the window where starlight woke him for school.

He closed his eyes and imagined he was
home, and a tiny tear rolled down his face.

Mrs. Opossum understood how Chester felt.
"Would you like to go home?" she whispered.
Chester nodded. "Yes, please."

"My neighbor Mrs. Rabbit will walk you home,"
she told him. "Thank you for coming to Pepper's
overday."

"Thank you for inviting me," yawned Chester.

When Chester arrived home, he jumped into his mother's arms. Mrs. Raccoon wrapped him in a huge, welcoming hug! "Thank you for bringing him home," she told Mrs. Rabbit and then carried Chester up into his very own hollow.

Chester curled up in his mother's lap, nestled
into her soft, cozy fur, and breathed in her familiar,
comforting scent.

"Are you angry that I came home
early?" he asked her.

Mrs. Raccoon gave Chester a
gentle squeeze. "Ronny and
I missed you so much,
you came home just in
time. But did you enjoy
Pepper's overday?"

YAWN

"Uh-huh," whispered Chester. Then he fell fast asleep, dreaming of his day spent with friends, knowing he was back in his mother's loving arms.

CHESTER'S OVERDAY POEM

Chester Raccoon came over to play.
He played with friends he saw each day.
He climbed some trees.
He fished for fish.
He had more fun than he could wish.
But when he closed his eyes that day
In a strange tree hollow far away,
He knew that something wasn't right.
Mommy Raccoon was out of sight.
Chester Raccoon looked sad and said
That he would like to go to bed
In his own tree hollow across the way,
And thanked his friend for a lovely day.

-A.P.